Hey Jack!

The Winning Goal
published in 2012 by
Hardie Grant Egmont
Ground Floor, Building 1, 658 Church Street
Richmond, Victoria 3121, Australia
www.hardiegrantegmont.com.au

A CiP record for this title is available from the National Library of Australia

Design by Stephanie Spartels
Typesetting by Michaela Stone

Printed in Australia by Griffin Press, an Accredited ISO AS/NZS 14001:2004 Environmental Management System printer.

7 9 10 8 6

The paper this book is printed on is certified against the Forest Stewardship Council® Standards. Griffin Press holds FSC chain of custody certification SGS-COC-005088. FSC promotes environmentally responsible, socially beneficial and economically viable management of the world's forests.

The Winning Goal

By Sally Rippin

Illustrated by Stephanie Spartels

hardie grant EGMONT

Can't stop grinning
Feels like he might burst
Fingers and toes tingling
Bouncy Mood

This is Jack.

He is in a bouncy mood.

It is his first day at soccer.

Jack is wearing his

new team uniform.

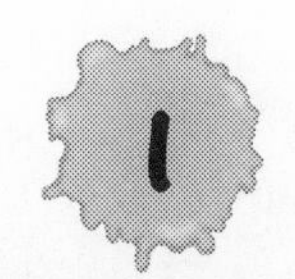

He is wearing bright orange soccer boots with real studs. Jack chose them himself. Jack has a shiny new soccer ball under his arm. He feels very **excited**.

Jack has been practising soccer all week in the backyard.

He practised dribbling
and passing and
shooting goals.

Jack is good at
dribbling. He is good
at passing too.
But most of all, Jack is
good at kicking goals.

Jack really hopes that
he will kick a goal today.

GOAL

'All right, team!'
calls the coach.
'Time to warm up.
I will watch you practise.
Then I will choose your
positions for the match.'

Jack and the other players
stand in a line facing
the coach. The coach
kicks the ball to them
one at a time.

Soon it will be Jack's turn.

Excited feelings

and nervous feelings

jumble around

in his tummy.

Jack swings his leg back and does a perfect kick – right into the coach's hands!

'Hey, Jack, good kick!' says the coach.

Jack grins proudly.

Next it is time to practise passing. The coach gives everyone a partner.

Jack's partner is called Jamal. He is even **bouncier** than Jack!

'Hey, Jack!' he says. 'You can call me Jem. Everyone does. Cool boots!'

Jack grins. 'Thanks, Jem,' he says.

Jack and Jem pass the
ball back and forwards
between them.

'Good work, boys!' says the coach. Jem gives Jack a high five. Jack likes Jem already.

Lastly, it is time to practise throwing and catching. Jack and Jem throw the ball to each other. Jack doesn't drop the ball once!

Today is a good day,
Jack thinks. He is sure
he will kick a goal today.

'Nice work,
Jack,' says the
coach. 'I think
I'll make you
our goalie.
We need someone good
at catching to play goalie.'

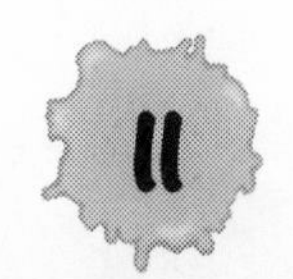

Goalie! Jack thinks.
I don't want to be goalie.
You can't kick a goal if
you're the goalie!

Jack hangs his head.
This is not such a
good day after all!

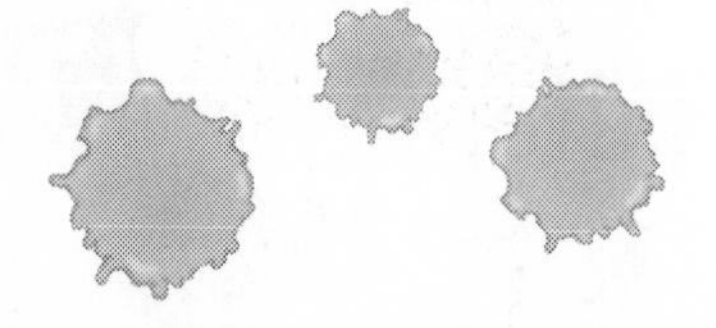

Jack stands between
the goal posts.
His bouncy feeling has
disappeared.

Now he feels as flat
as soccer ball with
no air inside it.

Being a goalie is boring, Jack thinks. He doesn't want to just stand around waiting for the ball. He wants to score a goal.

Jem has been put mid-field. Jack watches him dribble the ball around the other team's players.

He is right near the goal at the other end.

Then Jem kicks
the ball towards
the net.

It's a goal!

Everyone in the
team cheers. Jack is
happy for Jem, but
he wishes it was him
who had kicked a goal.

It's not fair, thinks Jack.

He feels like he's

been standing there

forever.

And the ball hasn't

come his way once!

He kicks a clod of grass.

'Jack! Hey, Jack!'

Jack looks up just in time to see the ball fly over his head. Straight into the net!

Oh no! It's a goal for the other team – and Jack let it in!

'Sorry!' Jack says in a squeaky voice.

'Eyes on the game, Jack,' the coach says kindly. But the other players in Jack's team look **annoyed**.

Even Jem won't look at him.

Of course he's annoyed with me, Jack thinks. *That was an easy save. Nobody will cheer for me now!*

Jack takes a deep breath. He squeezes his eyes together to stop any tears coming out. He won't cry in front of his new soccer team.

Now Jack keeps
his eyes glued to
the game. He watches
his team work hard to
keep the ball away
from the other players.
He watches as they try
to kick another goal.

But it's no use.
The other goalie
is too good.

It looks like

the game is going

to be a draw.

As Jack watches,

he notices something.

That goalie always jumps

up to save the goal,

he thinks. *I bet if I kicked*

low, I could get a ball right

through his legs!

But it's no use. A goalie can't kick goals.

Chapter Three

Now both teams have one goal each and the game is nearly over.

Jack sees a big boy in the other team get the ball.

He is coming towards Jack. It's the same boy who scored a goal last time.

No way! Jack thinks. *I'm not letting the ball in this time.*

The boy swings his leg back and takes a **mighty** kick.

The ball soars high
into the sky. It flies
straight towards the net!

Jack jumps high.
He stretches out
his hands – and
catches the ball!

Jack's team-mates
go wild. Jem jogs
over and gives Jack
a high five.

'Hey, Jack! That was awesome!' he says. 'Good save.'

'Thanks,' says Jack, grinning. Jem turns to run into the middle but Jack calls him back.

'Hey, Jem!' he says.

'What is it?' says Jem, jogging back.

'Shoot between the goalie's legs,' says Jack.

Jem looks at Jack and **frowns**.

‘What?’ he says.

‘Trust me,’ says Jack. ‘I’ve been watching him. Pretend you’re shooting high, but really shoot low.’

‘OK,’ says Jem. ‘I’ll give it a go.’

Jem runs into the middle of the field.

The match starts again.

Jack sees Jem get the ball. He dribbles it down the field towards the goal at the other end. Then he **kicks** it hard.

The other team's goalie jumps up, but the ball stays low.

It spins into the net –

right between the

goalie's legs!

Just like Jack

said it would.

Jack's whole team

cheers.

The whistle blows.

It's the end of the game.

Jack's team has won!

Jack is happy for Jem.

He has kicked two goals.

He helped their team

win the match.

Jack runs up to congratulate his new friend. Jem is surrounded by all the other players. They are **cheering** and clapping him on the back.

'Good kick!' one boy says to Jem.

‘Actually, that was Jack’s idea,’ Jem says.

‘He told me to

kick the ball low.’

Jack grins. ‘Yeah, but

you kicked the goal,’

he says to Jem.

Jem pats Jack on the

back. ‘We make a

good team,’ he says.

‘You all make a good

team,’ says the coach.

'Jack, you did a great job as goalie. Next week we'll have to get you out there kicking goals!'

Jack grins and nods. He can't wait until next week's match.

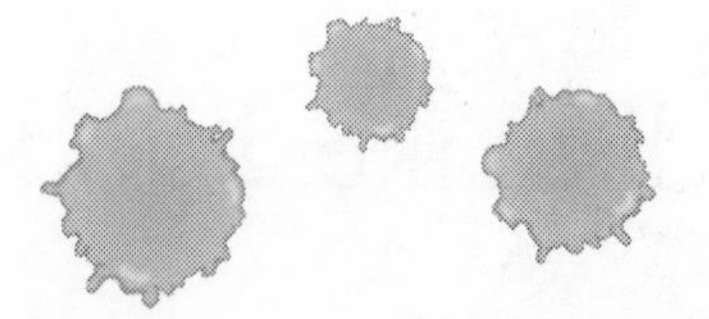

Goal!

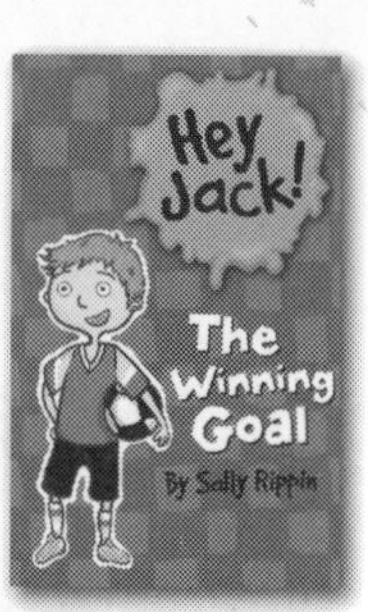

Collect them all!